MONSTER TRUCKS
BOLT
SPEED - 100
BRAINS - 72
POWER - 65
SKILL - bravery
Bolt loves nothing more than racing and will do anything for his monster mates – except their homework!
MONSTER TRUCKS
FIZZ
SPEED - 99
BRAINS - 65
POWER - 30
SKILL - fast loop-the-loops
Step aside, here's Fizz! Small but speedy, Fizz is three-time winner of the Trucksville Drift & Style Cup.
MONSTER TRUCKS
NEWTON
SPEED - 95
BRAINS - 100
POWER - 42
SKILL - speaks 60 languages
Newton's brain is more powerful than a top-notch computer and he has a stylish crash helmet.

MONSTER TRUCKS
CHUNK
SPEED - 91
BRAINS - 22
POWER - 100
SKILL - pie-eating champion
Everyone loves Chunk! His brain is the size of a ping pong ball but he has a heart of pure gold.
MONSTER TRUCKS
ROXY
SPEED - 98
BRAINS - 89
POWER - 64
SKILL - skatepark champion
Streetwise Roxy is the queen of the skatepark and can successfully land a triple backflip.
MONSTER TRUCKS
MASHER
SPEED - 100
BRAINS - 67
POWER - 76
SKILL - cheeky pranks
Loud, fast and rather smelly, Masher is everyone's favourite bad boy. But not when he bends the rules...

**For my three little monsters,
Darcy, George and Herbie
J.H.**

**To the big ones, the small ones, the hairy ones,
the scary ones, all our monster friends worldwide!
TADO**

First published in 2015 by Scholastic Children's Books
Euston House, 24 Eversholt Street
London NW1 1DB
a division of Scholastic Ltd
www.scholastic.co.uk
London ~ New York ~ Toronto ~ Sydney ~ Auckland
Mexico City ~ New Delhi ~ Hong Kong

PB ISBN 978 1407 14696 6

Printed in Malaysia

1 3 5 7 9 10 8 6 4 2

Mountain Rescue

Written by Jon Hinton
Illustrated by TADO

SCHOLASTIC

Today was the day of the **Monster Truck Party**, and Bolt, Roxy, Chunk, Fizz and Newton were on their way. They were having a great time racing along when they shot past the rather naughty Monster Truck named Masher.

"Help!" yelled Masher from the side of the road.
SCREETCH. The Monster Trucks slammed on their brakes.
"What's wrong?" asked Fizz.

"Absolutely **nothing**," laughed Masher and sped off, spraying them all with mud.

The five muddy friends continued their journey.

"Next up," announced Newton, "we climb the Huge Rocky Mountains."

The Monster Trucks stood gaping at the mountain range.
"It's too **high**," gasped Chunk. "We'll never make it to the top."
"Of course we will," replied Fizz. "We just need to keep moving forward one wheel at a time."
And so the five monster mates started their journey up, up, up...

They were halfway up the mountain when they found Masher at the side of the path – again.

"There's something wrong with my engine," whined Masher. "I don't have enough power to make it to the top. Can you help?"

Never one to leave a monster stranded, Chunk used every bit of his strength to pull Masher **all the way** to the very top.

"Let's **never**... do anything... like that... **ever**... again," panted an exhausted Chunk as they reached the peak. As soon as Chunk released his hook, Masher shot off. "Thanks for the lift," he cackled.

"I don't **believe** it," huffed Bolt. "There was **nothing** wrong with him. He tricked us again!"
"Don't worry," replied Roxy. "I've just spotted something which will cheer us up..."

"WHEEEEEEEEEEEEEEEEEEEEE!" yelled the five monsters as they hopped on skis, snowboards and sledges and flew down the mountain.

"This is the **best adventure** ever!" shrieked Roxy.

The five monster mates were making up for lost time.
"Are we there yet?" panted Chunk.
"Almost," said Newton. "We just have to cross Phoenix River and we'll be at the party."

They were midway across the bridge when... who did they bump into? Yes, that's right – **Masher.**

"My wheel's stuck," cried Masher. "Can you help me?"

Now, usually the Monster Trucks would never leave another monster in trouble. But Masher had tricked them twice already and they weren't going to fall for his pranks yet again. So the five monster mates continued across the bridge without stopping.

They had just reached the other side of the bridge when ...
RUMMMMMBBBBBBBLLLLE!
Hurtling across the bridge behind them was a huge, loud and fast Monster Train.
"Help me!" yelled Masher.

"Oh no!" gasped Bolt. "Masher really IS stuck!"

With clouds of smoke **billowing** out of its nostrils,
the Monster Train was gaining on Masher – and fast.

ROAR. Bolt raced across the bridge...
SHOVE. Bolt pushed Masher, freeing his wheel from the hole...
ZOOM. The two Monster Trucks darted back towards the others.

WHOOSH. In the nick of time, Bolt and Masher safely shot off the bridge, as the Monster Train rushed past. HOORAY!

"Thanks for rescuing me, Bolt!" said a very grateful Masher. "I'm **really** sorry for playing those tricks on you all."

“That’s ok,” replied Bolt. “The important thing is that we are all safe. Now, **let’s party...**”

Monster Truck

Party

MONSTER TRUCKS
BOLT
SPEED - 100
BRAINS - 72
POWER - 65
SKILL - bravery
Bolt loves nothing more than racing and will do anything for his monster mates – except their homework!
MONSTER TRUCKS
FIZZ
SPEED - 99
BRAINS - 65
POWER - 30
SKILL - fast loop-the-loops
Step aside, here's Fizz! Small but speedy, Fizz is three-time winner of the Trucksville Drift & Style Cup.
MONSTER TRUCKS
NEWTON
SPEED - 95
BRAINS - 100
POWER - 42
SKILL - speaks 60 languages
Newton's brain is more powerful than a top-notch computer and he has a stylish crash helmet.

MONSTER TRUCKS
CHUNK
SPEED - 91
BRAINS - 22
POWER - 100
SKILL - pie-eating champion
Everyone loves Chunk! His brain is the size of a ping pong ball but he has a heart of pure gold.
MONSTER TRUCKS
ROXY
SPEED - 98
BRAINS - 89
POWER - 64
SKILL - skatepark champion
Streetwise Roxy is the queen of the skatepark and can successfully land a triple backflip.
MONSTER TRUCKS
MASHER
SPEED - 100
BRAINS - 67
POWER - 76
SKILL - cheeky pranks
Loud, fast and rather smelly, Masher is everyone's favourite bad boy. But not when he bends the rules...

The End